The

Mysterious

Mansion

Part 2

By Hank Roberts

The Mysterious Mansion

Part II

PROLOGUE

This book is preceded by "The Mysterious Mansion". It is a continuation of that original story.

Marley and Allison Robbins, two energetic historians and investigative reporters, continue their lives living in an old mansion that they have refurbished. Many mysteries about the mansion have already been found, however the duo know that there are more to be discovered. Allison discovers, one evening, that one of the bedrooms in the mansion contains a locked and sealed closet, that no one has ever bothered to investigate. She knew that Nathan Greenwell lived in this bedroom and she knew that he was a man of many mysteries. What had he been working on for many years that caused him to be a recluse? How could his secrets about this home be disclosed? And, is there any such thing as time travel?

CHAPTER I

"Just a little to the right."

Marley stepped back to confirm his wife's impression of his hanging job. The picture, a 19th century rendering of Tom Greenwell, listed a bit to the left. He climbed back onto his footstool and realigned it. "Better?"

"Yes."

He looked over at Allie, the warmth of love radiating through his chest. He remembered the day he met her, two years before, within an hour of his arriving in town. She was so shy that she could barely look at him. With his first glance, he knew she'd be the one for him.

Looking around the home they'd built, he thanked God for bringing her into his life. Their restored 19th century home, the venerable Greenwell mansion, seethed with history, from its restored heavy furniture, huge marble fireplace, and immense crystal chandeliers, to the polished woodwork and winding staircase. Their artwork emphasized their shared interest in local history, maps, books and busts of local heroes.

On either side of the fireplace, portraits of the first two generations of Greenwells showed them in their long flock coats. Thomas, the founder, was pictured standing in front of the house. Pictures of slaves picking cotton hung on one side of Tom's picture and racehorses that he had raised hung on the other. A picture of Daniel, Tom's son, standing in the town green beside a statue of himself, which was placed by the town in his honor, was hanging nearby. Nathan, the youngest of the Greenwells, never posed for a portrait, nor a photograph.

Turning back to his wife, he noted that, as usual, she had her nose buried in a book. "What are you reading, dear?"

She showed him the cover, a paperback called *The Mysterious Mansion*. "It's a ghost story set in an old mansion. Interesting because of our own ghosts." She set the book on the table and took a sip of the coffee that was sitting in front of her. "I like books where the author describes life in the past. It seems so real, so fetching. Wouldn't it be wonderful if we could go there?"

"Where?"

"You know, the 19th century when the Greenwells lived and inhabited this mansion. We could interview them and see how they lived back then."

Allison and Marley Robbins lived very comfortably in their refurbished mansion. They both were extremely interested in historical facts and they enjoyed living in an old historic plantation house. The residents of their small town had accepted the fact that the old Greenwell mansion was not actually haunted. It did have its share of mysteries, but the townsfolk were ready to accept the Robbins, their weird lifestyle, and the old mansion.

Because of the gold found under Bobby Greenwell's grave, the Robbins had no worries about finances or maintaining a comfortable lifestyle. Marley did enjoy going, periodically, to Montgomery and appear on the TV station there. He kept his job as investigative reporter but he would not accept a salary. His main intention was to stay in the view of the public so he might promote any further historical discoveries that he or Allie might make.

Both Allie and Marley enjoyed making presentations to college and social groups. They were offered payment for their appearances, however they would give it back to the institution hosting the presentation, to be used for scholarships for history majors. History, archaeology, anthropology, they were all the same to this couple. They enjoyed promoting the education of those who chose to study these subjects. The Robbins would encourage the winners of the scholarships they set up and encouraged them to be open minded. They promoted the idea that "Anything could be there, if only one would look hard enough."

Marley and Allison enjoyed spending time in Tuscaloosa, at the University of Alabama, where there was a large library chock full of history books, especially about the South. The library was a wonderland for any historical investigative reporter, especially these two. Because of their notoriety, they were afforded access to the entire library, along with its many research capabilities. Marley and Allie would often praise the well-equipped library and its extremely helpful staff.

On one visit to the library, Allie discovered an article that told of Nathan Greenwell, Daniel's son. It was noted that Nathan had very dark skin and prominent Negro features. This boy could not be accepted as a son of Daniel and a slave so at the age of two he was sent off to England where he lived in a boarding school. Daniel had sufficient money to afford to keep Nathan in England, at least as long as Daniel lived. Daniel would, however, visit Nathan each spring and bring him gifts and news of life on the Greenwell plantation.

Nathan received a very intensive education. He was fluent in several languages and was proficient in math and physics. After graduating from college, Nathan worked for a short time in

England as a mechanical and physical engineer.

When Daniel died, Nathan was 23. He decided to return to the old Greenwell plantation, where he was born, even though he believed due to his skin color he would not be welcomed by the local residents. He vowed to live the life of a recluse within the mansion.

CHAPTER 2

Since Tuscaloosa was only an hour drive from their home, Allison would often find herself visiting the library several times a week. She had something specific that she was very interested in researching. Here at the University was an ideal location with its wealth of stored knowledge about many topics for Allie to delve as deep as she pleased into any particular subject.

Her mind couldn't help but wander to thoughts about the strange objects that she and Marley had found on the shelf above Nathan's bed. What was the purpose of the Ouija board? What was it there for and who used it? And there was no apparent reason for the bag that contained 24 different tiles, each containing one strange letter. There must have been some logical reason for the presence of these items. But what?

As Allison conducted her in depth research into the objects that were found in Nathan's room, she was cautious not to arouse the interest or suspicion of any of the workers in the library. They already thought that she was a little touched, but Allie didn't want any further inquiries.

"Ok," said Allison to herself. "All I have to do is research a few simple objects. A Ouija board, a set of runes, a crystal ball, a metallic spherical ball, and a voodoo doll. What could be easier than that?"

When the runes were researched, it was found that they were a set of 24 stones. On each of these stones was inscribed a single letter. These letters were used to create words before the Greek alphabet was accepted for common use. Allie could not determine any possible use for these stones by Nathan Greenwell. He could read and write in English, French, and Latin. Why would he want to rely on an archaic set of outdated letters? She knew that the voodoo doll was often used to place spells and hexes on other unsuspecting persons. The crystal ball was often used by those who claimed to be able to see into the future. No substantial evidence could be located to prove that it was anything more than a crystal sphere.

The Ouija board was found to be a spiritual type medium, through which the user could gain answers to questions that were otherwise unanswerable. This type of device, related to witchcraft and sorcery, was most often used by people of a dark spiritual nature.

The metallic spherical structure required more extensive research. When Allie approached the librarians with the subject of a metallic sphere, she was guided to hundreds of various locations to research. Her research led her to topics of perpetual motion, space travel, time travel, energy production and many others. As she read through the many references, she continued to think back on how any of these uses would be used by or effect the life of Nathan Greenwell.

She realized that Nathan would have been exposed to stories about time travel and even perpetual motion. Many scientists of his day had been experimenting with these subjects. None of them had devised a reasonable means by which their ideas could be proven, of course. Many of the inventors and scientist also delved into alchemy, again without success. There were so very many things that stimulated the curiosity of the people of the early 1900s, very few of which were ever proven.

Marley was always excited to meet with Allie when she got home from Tuscaloosa. They would spend hours talking about the different finds that she had made during her research.

On one particular evening, Allison returned with some provocative news. She had found that it was believed, during the early 20th Century, that metallic spheres were related to, and used in, the development of time travel. Often the early researchers would put people in large spherical metal containers in an attempt to send them into another time dimension. This transformation could never be proven, but it was tested on more than one occasion by the scientists of that day. She also found that the letters inscribed in the 24 runes were supposed to be able to communicate with beings from ancient times, when encountered by any of the space travelers.

When this information was shared with Marley, both historians agreed on the fact that Nathan must have been researching some type of time travel. At least now they could pinpoint the direction in which their own research must proceed. Was there anything that they had overlooked, within the massive mansion?

The Robbins had found all of Nathan's possessions, which were very few. There was a rag doll, a spherical metal ball, a set of 24 tiles with some type of letter inscribed into them, and a Ouija board. There were some old clothes and slippers, all of which didn't amount to much.

CHAPTER 3

After long contemplations about everything that had been heard and found in their new home, Marley remembered that they had not bothered to remove the locks or investigate the small closet which was located in Nathan's bedroom. The closet was very small and didn't seem to be of any significance, however, with all of the other weird findings there was no telling what would be found within that closet. Certainly, it was worth taking a look.

With hammer, chisel, saw, and wire clippers in hand, the two curious investigators proceeded to Nathan's bedroom where they planned to open the door to the small closet. This closet was secured with several locks and some metal straps, which were bolted to the door and wall. Marley spent several hours sawing on the hard metal locks before finally cutting them off. The metal the locks were composed of seemed so strange, he decided to submit them for analysis to the science department at the University.

It took the couple a complete day to fully remove all the objects which secured this door. When they finally could look into the closet, all they could see was a small empty room. The dimensions were 3' X 5'. There were no clothes hangers nor any movable structures. There was only a dusty old room with wooden slats for the walls and floor. Nothing appeared to be odd or different about this small space. What could it have been used for and why was it so securely closed? This appeared to be another dimension of this mysterious mansion.

One-night Allison found it impossible to sleep. She woke Marley and told him of her recurring thoughts about the secret closet. "I must satisfy my curiosity about this mystery before it drives me insane," she told her husband. "I'm going to get up and see if I can find any more answers to our dilemma."

She slipped on some jeans and a floppy old denim shirt. Her slippers, which she put on, were right at the side of her bed. Allie left their bedroom and proceeded to the bedroom which had been occupied by Nathan.

When she turned on the light in Nathan's room, she heard a distinct swish of air that was coming from the small closet. She proceeded to the closet and opened the door, which had previously been locked tight. As she stood and observed the small space, she noticed a loose board on the floor, from which came the sound of escaping air. When she touched the board it moved slightly, allowing a dim beam of light to pass through.

"Where could that light be coming from?" Allie wondered.

Squatting down beside the loose board, Allison tried, in vain, to move it. It was securely attached but it was slightly loose. Her curiosity began to run away with her as she thought of the different ways that she might get the board to move and provide her with a view of what was beneath. The tension in her mind and body now grew to a great crescendo of excitement.

Allison stepped back to the shelf in the room where Nathan's objects of curiosity remained. In one hand she lifted the metal sphere and in the other she secured the odd-looking voodoo doll. Not knowing why, she chose these two items, she cautiously stepped back to the small closet.

It was hard for her to decide whether she should call for her husband to accompany her in this adventure. Marley would probably not be interested, unless she uncovered something that was really a showstopper. He had been exposed on many occasions to the mundane discoveries that they had made. Now it would take something really shocking to get his attention.

Alone and slightly trembling, Allie proceeded to the small dark closet. She placed the small voodoo doll in her shirt pocket. The head of the doll stuck out, as though the doll was watching her every move. With the metal sphere secure in both hands, Allison proceeded to a position which brought her directly over the loose board in the floor. Twisting and turning the metal structure, Allie tried to induce some type of response. Nothing happened.

She then stepped back out of the dark closet and into the light of the bedroom. There she turned the sphere in all types of positions, trying to see if there were any markings on it. After about two minutes of close scrutiny, Allie discovered an extremely small "N" stamped into one position on the ball. "I wonder what this N stands for?" she asked herself. "Did Nathan stamp it here to indicate that this was his possession? Was it stamped here to indicate what type metal was used in its construction? Perhaps it indicated the direction north."

Allison oriented herself in the room to determine the true position of north. She positioned her finger over the N on the ball and then reentered the closet. Standing directly over the loose board, she pointed the N toward magnetic north and held the sphere very still. The ball began getting warmer and warmer until it was difficult to hold. The closet floor trembled and a 2½' X 3' opening appeared, directly under her. There was a stairway that led down from the newly made opening in the floor. "Now where could this possibly lead?" she pondered.

Being the inquisitive investigator that she was, she cautiously began descending the stairs. When she reached the floor of the room beneath, faint voices could be heard coming from the adjacent room. Allison still had her bedroom slippers on so she could move silently across the floor and peek into the next room.

She observed that the adjoining room was a large dining room. There was a very large dining table where the entire Greenwell family sat dining. A stately, proper man, whom she suspected was

Tom Greenwell, sat in the massive chair at the end of the table. Allison could hear him barking out orders to his family members.

"Those 10 acres up by the house require cultivating and planting immediately, if we plan to have any decent truck patch for our meals and canning. The darkies already got their acre planted and its coming along fine. You boys take some of those pickneys with you and get that planting done."

Allison noticed a teenage servant moving away from the table and headed in her direction. She jerked back out of sight, knocking the voodoo doll out of her shirt pocket. It fell directly in the middle of the hallway. As the servant reached that area, she bent down and picked up the doll. "My dol," she exclaimed. "How in de worl dis cums to bees heae? Dis dol be missin fer bout a year now." The girl took the doll and proceeded around the corner where she ran directly into Allie.

"Ghoost," she tried to scream out. She was too frightened to say much of anything. Blood had rushed from her face and she had turned almost completely white. Allison hurried toward the girl and placed her hand over her mouth. "I'm not a ghost but a friendly visitor," Allie told the girl. "You must not tell anyone of our meeting, or I will come back and haunt you." The negro girl, trembling and dazed, squatted down beside the small table located there. "No mizz, I won tell no one lest they fetch me and beat me sometin terribl'."

As quickly and quietly as possible, Allison stepped back to the stairway, from which she had come. When reaching the top, she secured the metal sphere and turned the N toward true north. A trembling feeling once again encompassed the floor and the access to the lower level closed. She found herself, again, standing in the dark closet.

As Allie stood in the bedroom awe stricken, she contemplated what had just happened. This was an earth-shaking finding, but should she go directly and wake Marley and tell him? Perhaps not. Not until morning when they could both properly investigate this new mystery of their special mansion. She slipped quietly back into her and Marley's bedroom, removed her slippers, and snuggled back into bed, pulling up the covers.

"Boy do I have some news to share with my hubby when we wake up tomorrow," Allie whispered to herself as she drifted off to sleep.

CHAPTER 4

Allie and Marley woke up as the first ray of sunshine made its way through the pulled curtains in their bedroom. Marley saw the "mule eating briars" look on Allie's face. Before she could speak, he turned to her and said, "Whatever crazy discovery you have made will surely wait until we can get some breakfast."

They did their usual morning activities and dressed in comfortable clothes. Marley went outside to grab the daily newspaper and Allison went to the kitchen and began cooking eggs, bacon and "store bought" biscuits. She always wanted to make the biscuits that were made from scratch, but she never seemed to find the time.

Settled at the breakfast table and enjoying their first cup of coffee, Marley turned to his wife and said, "OK. I'm ready. Let's hear whatever great discovery you've made." Allie began babbling away with all of the details about the time warp closet.

"Slow down, slow down," Marley shouted. "I can hardly understand a word that you are saying. Start again from the point where you went to Nathan's bedroom last night."

Allie composed herself and explained in great detail all that she had experienced the preceding evening, including her brief visit to the 19th century.

After finishing her descriptions of the previous night's activities and pouring them both another cup of coffee, Allison gazed across the table to see what Marley had to say.

"I knew that there was more to Nathan's being a hermit than met the eye. He not only wanted to remain unseen, he wanted to keep his private research work a secret." Marley finished his coffee. "Sounds like we're ready for a new adventure!"

Before they would endeavor to make a journey to the Greenwell mansion of the 1800s, they agreed that they would like to take some gifts. They decided they had to remember that they would not be able to take something which would change the course of history. History, from the 1800s to the 2000s had already been established. People had lived their lives and situations had occurred that could not be changed.

Marley decided to secure a small amount of several different seeds for planting. He realized that agriculture had enjoyed many advancements and improvements since 1800. He researched the different types of crops that were being grown back in antebellum times and, using this information, he decided to collect some seeds of plants that weren't already being grown there. Marley collected a half pound small bag of different types of hybrid corn, some of which would grow much faster and produce higher yields than the corn that the Greenwells were currently growing. He also collected seeds for melons, squash, beans, beats, turnips and other vegetables that were regulars in the growing of a family garden. He figured these could help the Greenwells without changing the path of history. He placed the seeds in individual plastic bags and secured them in the back pouch of a jacket that he planned to wear on their journey.

Allison was just as picky about choosing something that she could take that would not affect future historical events. She would have liked to have been able to inform Bobby about the fact that his brother was going to kill him, but that would have altered history. She would also have liked to warn them of the impending war between the states, which was soon coming and would affect the lives of all Americans. Allie had to move away from these thoughts and think of something that she could take that would be valued in their time of history.

Finally, she decided to work toward taking something that would be used and appreciated by the ladyfolk of that time period. She knew that they could already sew and they knew how to make their own clothes. Cooking and canning were skills used by these people for future meals and for their simple necessities of living. What they didn't possess was different cosmetics, especially perfumes. When a girl married during that time, the only thing that was used to create a pleasant smell for the ladies was for her to carry a bunch of freshly picked flowers. Often friends would fix for the bride a small bundle of fresh flowers that she could wear under her outer clothing to improve the under washed body aroma.

Allison picked out items that were made in Paris and other European cities, where she was sure the Greenwells had no contact. She also included a few lipsticks, rouges, and scented body powders.

Allie's gift items were packed into a small canvas duffle bag, which she could easily throw over her shoulder. Inside of this small bag, she also packed a couple of changes of clothes. She didn't include particularly fancy outfits, since she realized that many of the ladies of the 1800s only owned one fancy dress and maybe two sets of work clothes. The couple wanted to fit into the pattern of life of the people who lived where they were going.

On the morning of their departure, the couple dressed in some work clothes, which were comprised of denim from top to bottom, low top used tennis shoes, and beat up baseball caps from different teams. Filled with excitement and wonder, they headed to Nathan's bedroom to try and reproduce Allie's adventure.

Marley secured the sphere and examined it, locating the N that Allie had told him about. The two explorers entered the small closet with Allison holding her finger over the N embossed on the metal sphere, just as she had done the night before, so that she would know the direction of magnetic north.

As the couple stood directly over the loose board on the floor of the closet, Allie removed her finger from covering the N. Again, the floor trembled and an entrance way was exposed beneath their feet. As Allie had reported to Marley, there was a stairway leading down to the room below.

When they reached the bottom of the stairs, they could hear voices of several children playing. When they peered into the adjacent room, they saw several white children dressed in makeshift grey military uniforms playing with make believe swords. The black children were sitting in a crowded group, over in the corner, watching the others play.

Marley and Allison decided that it would be best if they were to leave the house through the back door and come around to the front to make a formal entrance. They both knew the layout of the entire house for it was the house in which they were currently living. The only real change was the difference in time. They found themselves firmly transfixed into the 1800s. Neither of them knew how they would be received by the Greenwell family when they approached the front door and introduced themselves. Allie said, "You know the saying, nothing ventured nothing gained."

When the Robbins reached the front of the house, they found Tom Greenwell and two of his cousins sitting in three large rocking chairs on the front veranda.

"Let me do the talking," Marley whispered to Allison. "In these days the men usually did all the talking." Allie glanced back at him with a sarcastic expression on her face.

"Morning gentlemen. Are you the men of the house?" Marley blurted out. "My wife and I are investigative reporters and we would like to write an article about life on this plantation. If you would afford us this great pleasure, we will be happy to include you in any articles about the mansion that might be published."

The men seemed quite shocked at what seemed to them as very odd visitors. One of them spilled his iced tea onto the floor as he jumped back from the intrusive visitors. Mr. Tom

Greenwell was a gentleman who was always desirous of special attention and this notoriety was something that pleased him very much. He invited the couple to come up onto the porch and enjoy some fresh sweet tea with him and his cousins.

There were eight large Corinthian columns supporting the huge porch, the first floor of the mansion, and the roof of the second floor. Leading up to the porch were twelve wide wooden steps, lined with huge decorative wooden banisters. The house, the banisters and the railings were all stark white, trimmed in bright green. The floor of the porch was a light grey, which helped disguise the many scuff marks from heavy work boots.

Once the Robbins were seated in their smaller rockers on the porch, they could easily view the massiveness of the great plantation. One of the black servants was called upon to bring two more glasses of tea. The group sat on the veranda for at least an hour engaging in small talk about the nearby farmers, the number of darkies that were present, the soon to be planted crops, and the weather. Tom inquired as to where Marley and Allie were staying and when he received the answer that they weren't exactly sure, he demanded that they stay there at the "big house." Marley immediately accepted and stated that this would give them even more time to interview Tom and his family.

From their viewpoint, there on the porch, Marley and Allie could clearly see a gravel road that led up to the house. On both sides of this road there were massive fields being worked by the slaves. There were 8 to 10 mules in each of the fields and at least 30 black workers plowing and planting. Each mule was hitched to, and drawing, a single plow which was driven by a black man. Black women followed behind the plows, each carrying and planting the different crop that was to be planted in that field. The smaller field to the right, as they were told by Tom, was being cultivated for growing vegetables, along with watermelons. There were about 165 acres on this side of the road. They were being planted with corn, different beans, collard greens, cucumbers, squash, turnips (along with their turnip greens), and other common crops.

The field on the left side was reserved for cotton. There was a total of 1,200 acres which were planted with this extremely profitable commodity. Behind the house was a smaller garden of only five acres, known as the family's truck patch, which contained watermelons and cantaloupes to be consumed by the family. There was a variety of fruit trees located all over the plantation. There was even 10 acres of pecan trees, which yielded a plethora of delicious nuts in the fall of each year.

CHAPTER 5

Tom Greenwell called out to one of his maid servants, "Mattie…get yourself in the back and kill some chickens. We need to fry up some special meal for our guests. Make some chitlin, corn bread, collards, and sweet taters – and make up a new batch of that sweet tea. I see Daniel and Bobby comin' up the road. They been supervising the darkies and I'll bet they are plenty hungry."

Mattie, a robust black slave girl about 25 years old, appeared from within the mansion. "Yessir, massa Tom. I bees fryin' dem chicken up directly." Looking directly at Tom's guests, Mattie said, "Doz y'all wants sum mo' dat sweet tea?" All the guests declined a refill.

All of the family, including the two cousins and the Robbins, sat at the large dining room table. It had been immaculately set and was being served by five of the house slave girls, who were all properly dressed in their uniforms. As one of the younger girls entered the room, Allie noticed that under her white tied belt was the doll which Allison had dropped on her first visit. This girl must have been the one who saw a ghost. She didn't recognize Allie, and she went on with her normal serving to the table.

After grace was said and the food was served, Tom began the table conversation. "Y'all gonna stay for a spell, aren't ya? We got plenty of plantation to show ya in the next couple of days." Tom's cousins were planning to leave the next morning. They had a long trip back to Virginia.

Tom was proud of his plantation and he wanted for his visiting reporters to be able to witness, firsthand, the activities that went on at the Greenwell plantation. Tom said to Daniel, his oldest son, "I want you and Bobby to fetch a buggy and take Mr. Marley 'round the property for a good close look at the goings on."

Daniel, begrudgingly, said "Why I gotta take that liberal minded brodder of mine? He ain't nothin 'cept a pain in the ass."

Tom replied in a rather stern voice, "You do what you're told, boy. I ain't 'lowing no squabbling twinx you two."

Sarah, Tom's wife, and Allison were sitting together at the far end of the table.

They were becoming quite attached to each other. Sarah offered to show Allie around the house, the staff, the canning process, and all of the womanly functions of running the house. She also offered to allow Allie to watch as the slave girls prepared the food for the family. Baking chitlin and corn bread and properly spicing and cooking greens, field peas and the like was something that was a special talent, possessed only by finely trained servants. They were the only ones allowed to do the cooking. The other girls tended to housekeeping and serving the meals.

As the maid servant who had the voodoo doll in her apron came close, Allie asked where she had gotten it. "Dar be a ghoos dat visited," said the girl. "She musta drapped it cuz I seed it on de flo. It bees mine, sept it be lost ever since a nudder ghoos visit a whilst ago." Allie realized that she was referring to Nathan's visit previously. Time here seemed so different. It had been years since Nathan had made his appearance there. The girl referred to it as though it was just a few weeks ago.

Daniel Greenwell, who was quite an activist and always wanting to start a controversial discussion, said, "Them damn Yankees are still trying to stir up trouble for us Southerners. Now they wantin' ta make us give up our slaves. Let them come down and raise all their precious cotton and see who would have to do all the work. I ain't plowing dem fields or choppin' dat cotton."

Tom spoke up and told Daniel to keep his comments about political matters to himself. Their visitors were here to see the functioning of a plantation, not get bogged down in local political ideas. "Leave them damn Yankees alone for the time being," Tom said.

After dinner everyone was served a generous slice of fresh apple pie. Neither of the investigators had ever tasted pie as good. Allie told Sarah that she wanted the girls to teach her how to bake that way. "Tomorra I's gwin show ya all da cookin' I does," said Mattie, who appeared to be the head of all the house servants.

Marley noticed that all of the silverware, china, and crystal that they ate with was the same as he and Allison had found deserted in the old mansion. There was no comment about it, but there were many things that the visiting couple recognized, such as paintings and furniture. When they were shown to their bedroom, they acted like they didn't know the way. The accommodations were excellent, except for the lack of a bathroom. They both settled in for a good night's sleep.

In the early hours of the morning they were awakened by the loud crowing of several roosters. The sun was just rising over the horizon and breakfast had already been prepared. Allison and Marley slipped back on the clothes they had on the day before and made their way down to the dining room for a hot morning meal. There were warmed over beans and cornbread, along with grits, bacon, fresh biscuits with homemade jam, and fried eggs. Now they realized why everyone was a bit overweight. Who could eat like this all the time?

After everyone had finished breakfast and the maids began cleaning up from the meal, there was a bit of time that allowed Allison and Marley to present the Greenwells with the small gifts that they had brought with them. The couple told the Greenwell family that they wanted to present some items to them and that they would like to meet back, in a few minutes, in the study where the presentations could be made.

Both of the visitors hurriedly went to their room and secured the gifts that they wanted to present. They went back down to the study, where they were met by the entire host family.

Marley started off, not to outdo Allie, but because men's business during those days always took precedence over women's concerns. He laid upon the table several small plastic zip lock bags. Just the sight of these bags astonished the observing family. They had never seen plastic, let alone self-sealing bags.

As Marley proceeded to open each of the bags, which were all labeled with the type of seeds that they possessed, he explained the value of each of them. When Tom Greenwell saw the corn seeds, which Marley had told him would produce much more and more healthy corn, he immediately secured them and gave them to Daniel and instructed him to have the darkies fence in a special two-acre tract where these seeds could be planted. This way they could keep a close eye on them and if they were much superior to their corn, they would save the produced seeds for planting the following year. "If these corn seeds do what you say they will do," said Tom to Marley, "we would have a much larger yield from our crop, even if grown on the same amount of land. We could easily increase our profits from this corn by a large bit. I won't know until next year when the harvest comes in if I should thank you."

Mr. Robbins explained about the various seeds that he had brought. Sarah Greenwell assured Marley that they would create a special test garden, up close to the house, for the planting of these other seeds. They were all excited about seeing the products that would be produced by planting these new hybrid seeds. They had to plant them close to the house to keep the cattle, yard animals, and deer from eating the tender sprouts.

After Marley finished, it was Allie's turn to make her presentations. She took out her bag that contained perfume, powder, and lipstick. When she opened the first bottle of French perfume, Sarah screeched with joy. Allie dabbed a little on her finger and placed it behind Sarah's ear. The wonderful fragrance filled the entire room. The visitor then took out some body powder and brushed it onto the face of her hostess. With a small amount of lipstick, used for rouge on her cheeks, and a little on her lips,

Sarah's appearance was completely changed. Tom blurted out, "My God what a beautiful lady. And she's my wife."

Tom was asked if he approved of the changes that had been made to his wife. "Damn straight I approve. I ain't never seen her look that pretty nor smell that good. I can't wait for us to have company over so I can show her off." Tom added, "The governor and his wife are coming to visit next month, and I would appreciate it if Allie would show her how to make herself up that pretty. Everyone will be so very impressed. Shoot, she's prettier than a newborn mule."

After the presentations, Allison was led off to follow Sarah on a tour of the entire plantation home. She was shown the cooking area along with where the wood for the stove was stored. Outside the back door there was a large water trough where dishes were washed. Another trough stood beside the washing trough. This one was for storing drinking water. There was a path outside the back door that led about 50 feet to the living quarters for the house servants. Behind that was a small outhouse for use by the slaves. To the left, and more closely located to the big house, was a larger outhouse for the Greenwells and their guests.

There was a large chicken pen and coop where eggs were collected daily. There were also several free-range chickens running around the yard. In the corner of the pen was a tree stump that was used as a chopping block for removing the chickens' heads. Beside it was a large iron pot for scalding the dead chickens and removing their feathers.

Two black men were in a small field near the house plowing and planting the truck patch where the household vegetables and melons were to be grown. There was activity all around. Everyone had a specific job to do, and they were all busy doing that to which they were assigned. Sarah called out to the two black men and told them that she wanted a special garden placed up close to the main house to grow the new seeds that they had just received.

"Yes ma'am. We be comin' up there directly. We get rite on dat job fer ya," was called out by one of the men.

Daniel and Bobby pulled up to the front of the mansion with two horses attached to a small flatbed wagon. They had come to pick up Marley to take him on a tour of the plantation. One of the servants brought out a sealed jar of tea and six sandwiches. "Y'all gwin be gon fer a bit. Ya maw said y'all gwinna need som food fo y'all get bak." Bobby took the food and drink and secured it for the buggy ride, which in some places would be quite bumpy.

CHAPTER 6

Marley donned a large broad brimmed straw hat to prevent the sun from burning the back of his neck and shoulders, like it did on many of the farm and plantation workers, thus causing those who saw them to call them "red necks."

Before the buggy had gotten away from the mansion, Daniel and Bobby began arguing. Bobby was a small, frail young man while Daniel was much larger. Daniel usually ended up winning the arguments. They continued to argue most of the day as they traveled throughout the plantation. There were no large disputes. They just couldn't get along with each other. Marley recalled how it was suggested, based on findings at the mansion in much later years, that Daniel had killed Bobby and hid his body away behind the large fireplace. Now the motives of this murder seemed to becoming clear and understandable.

About a mile down the dusty road they came to their first stop. It was a row of about twenty-five very small shack cottages in a single row. Each of the houses had a small fireplace with a poorly constructed brick chimney. There was a small front porch on about 5 or 6 of the shacks. The porch was not elevated, it just protruded out from the house. The walls were all made of roughhewn wood planks, many of which did not fit together tightly, causing cracks to appear in the sides. The floors of all the shacks were dirt and there was only one room per house. The inside dimensions were about 12 X 14 feet and all the individual families had to make this space do as their living domain.

Outside of each cabin was a small area in which they could build a fire for cooking. Behind the shacks stood three fairly large outhouses, which were shared by all of the families. There were several black children who were running around outside the houses. All of the children were being supervised by two black women, who rotated their responsibilities each week. The women were needed more for working the fields than babysitting.

At the far end of the row of houses was a small vegetable garden which was fenced with split logs and leftover lumber. This garden was maintained by all of the slaves and it produced food that they all could share. The bigger the man of the family was, the larger share of vegetables his family would receive.

There was never more than enough to go around, but it seemed adequate to feed them all.

The cabin row was located on about two acres of cleared land. About 50 feet behind the cabins was the beginning of large trees and an extensive forest. There were four mangy, skinny dogs that had free range of the property, along with about twenty-five chickens and two pigs. Although the housing situation was much less desirable than that of the plantation owners, it seemed to fairly well fit the basic needs of the residents. When asked how many slaves lived in these cottages, Bobby and Daniel again started a big argument. They just couldn't get along or agree on anything.

Marley and his guides made their way down the dusty road until they came to ten extremely large fields. These fields were well over 100 acres each. The Greenwell family had found that they could manage the cotton better if it were planted in 100 acre plots. In the off seasons they would allow the cattle to roam freely in the various fields. The cow's droppings provided excellent fertilizer for the following year's crop.

These fields were all planted with cotton and they were tended by several slaves. Now that the cotton plants were up and growing, the slaves had to constantly chop the cotton fields to keep the weeds out. Growing cotton appeared to be a continuous job, from the tilling of the soil to the planting of the seeds. From there the new plants had to be kept up and see that no weeds choked them out. After the cotton was mature, it had to be harvested, weighed, and sent to the gin. The old used plants would then be cut down and plowed into the soil to nourish it until the next planting season. It was no wonder that it took an army of workers to keep up with the entire process of raising cotton. Although many cotton fields were planted near a water source, there was rarely any irrigation to be worried about. Rain and mother nature were the only factors that were considered in enhancing the crops.

A couple of miles down the road the trio located several medium sized fields, each approximately 10 acres each. These fields were used for growing corn, soybean, squash, beans, and potatoes. One section, about an acre large, was set aside for watermelons. All of the crops that were not consumed by the plantation owners and their families were taken into the local towns and communities and sold at the market.

When the travelers reached an area where there were several slaves working a field, Daniel pulled their wagon to a stop. He got out and approached the workmen. "I want y'all to block off half of one of these 10-acre fields and prepare it specially for growing a special kind of corn," Daniel told them. "Y'all going to have to look out special for this field. We are gonna weigh the corn yield and compare it to the corn that we have been growing. I'll bring you the special corn seeds when it is close to planting time."

Daniel, Bobby, and Marley stopped along the way for the group to have lunch and something to drink. They stopped in an area with several large hardwood trees that provided welcomed shade. This was a favorite location for the Greenwell family to host picnics. It was extremely lovely and peacefully relaxing. There was a small creek that ran close to their picnicking area, which made this entire small location seem like an oasis in the middle of a desert.

After leaving the rest area, they headed further down the road. It gently curved and the three on the viewing expedition, the two horses, and small wagon were now headed back in the direction of home. Along the way they came to a large field on which there were about 80 cows and 2 bulls. There were also several goats, and in one corner there was a pig sty where there lived 12 large pigs and 8 small ones. As the group passed, they could almost identify the animals by the pungent odor that was emitted. Marley was told that these animals were raised for the family to eat. The plantation did not raise cattle for sale at the markets. When there was an excess of animals born, the Greenwells would share a couple with the slaves, who always held a large barn fire/cook out and all enjoyed the welcomed feast.

To the side of the cow field was a fair size barn where hay was stored and cattle were sheltered in the extremely cold weather, which was very seldom here in the south. Inside the barn lived three wild cats, which were kept there to keep the mouse residents in the corn crib at bay.

The wagon headed back to the main house where a big dinner meal was being prepared. Marley was ready to get off the wagon, get a big cool drink of tea, and get away from the constant bickering between Daniel and Bobby.

CHAPTER 7

When Marley stepped back onto the large front porch of the mansion, he was greeted with a tall cold mint julip. He and Tom sat on the porch and rocked as Tom questioned Marley about his day touring the plantation. They discussed the several things that the Greenwell boys had taken him to see. He assured Tom that he had gathered quite enough information to take back home and write an interesting article, perhaps even a full book.

When Marley saw Tom puffing on a big cigar, he rushed up to his room where he had left some fine Cuban cigars that he had brought for his host. He quickly returned to the porch and presented the cigars to Tom, who immediately unwrapped one and lit it up.

"Damn these cigars are smooth. What state grew this fine tobaccee?" asked Tom.

"This tobacco was grown and the cigars processed in Cuba," stated Marley. "They are in great demand by many gentlemen."

"I can certainly see why," stated Tom. Both men relaxed back in their rocking chairs, enjoying their bourbon drink and their fine cigars.

The crisp sounds of the farm bell rang loud enough for anyone within a mile to hear. Mattie called out, "Y'all bees commin. Dinna gwin be served directly and Miss Allison and me been working ponst it all day, and I is shor it gwin be fine."

The entire family gathered around the splendidly set table. Tom said grace and the servants began bringing in the food. There were two large pheasants on one plate and about 10 quail on another. Mashed potatoes, butter beans, and gravy were also served. In the middle of the table was a large hand sliced loaf of homemade bread. The meal was nothing less than a feast, but this was the type of meal that was served to the Greenwells every day.

As they all set around the table, Marley mentioned that he and Allison would be going home the following day.

Sarah and Tom let out a sigh. "We have really enjoyed your company," said Sarah to her visitors.

"We have thoroughly enjoyed our visit," stated Marley, "but we must go back home and begin compiling all of the notes that we have gathered here on the plantation. Allie and I both feel that we have brought gifts to you that will change your entire lives. If you plant the various seeds that I have brought, and if they produce abundantly as I have told you they would, you may want to share some of the future seeds with friends and neighbors. This will give us a great feeling of accomplishment for having brought you such products. Future generations will prosper from the great advancements that you will make with these crops."

Allison smiled at Marley and said, "I can't wait until you taste the dessert that Mattie and I made. It is bread pudding topped with bourbon sauce. It contains crushed pecans and some preserved peaches. Mattie says that it is one of her specialties."

After dinner, one of the slave girls came over to the Robbins. "I's gwin be up ta ya room directly to gather your'n dirtee clooz. Y'all haz dem sittin outside da room and I gwin wash dem and fetch dem rite back outside yo doo." Allie was pleased to know that they would have clean clothes to wear home the next day.

When they had finished their meal, they all headed to their separate bedrooms. Although it was only 8:30, everyone here got to bed early and rose up with the chickens. Back in their room, Marley asked Allie if she thought that she needed to write down any notes about their visit.

"I don't think so," she said. "I have been so impressed and excited that I don't think I could forget anything that I saw."

The slave girl, Edna, came to pick up the dirty clothes. While she was there, Allison took her aside and told her that she wanted her to do a big favor for them.

Edna said, "Yessum, Miss Allie. Massa Tom don tol us ta do anything y'all had a reconing fer."

Allie told Edna that this must be a strict secret between the two of them. Edna understood.

The next morning at 3 am, before anyone else got out of bed, Edna came to the Robbins' bedroom, woke them up, and delivered their clean clothes. She then led them downstairs and into the small room, through which they had originally come. This room had been closed to the rest of the family since Marley and Allison arrived. The stairway leading up to the closet was still in place. Edna simply led them to the door of the room, but she did not come in, nor did she look inside.

The reporters hurried to the stairs that were awaiting them, scampered upstairs and into the small closet in Nathan's room, where they secured the metal sphere which they had left there, and oriented the N away from north. A small rumble occurred, and the stairs were removed from leading down and the floor securely closed back. There was no trace of their venturing through time. Marley led Allison back out of the closet and into the bedroom. They placed the metal sphere back on the shelf, from wince it had been taken, and they both headed back to their own bedroom where they would sleep the rest of the night and wake in the morning to some fascinating discussions.

Back at the Greenwell plantation, the family arose to find that their visitors had already gone. Both Sarah and Tom said that they would have liked to wish them goodbye. When they questioned if anyone had seen them get up and leave in the early morning, there was no reply.

"I guess they are just like us," said Tom. "They hate long partings. I do wish them well with their reports about our plantation."

CHAPTER 8

In the morning when Allison and Marley awoke, they looked at each other as if to say, "What the hell just happened?" They both slipped on lounging clothes and headed down to the kitchen for their first cup of coffee.

"This has been an amazing adventure," said Allie, "if I am to believe what I recently observed."

Marley settled her down by mentioning that they had observed many mysteries while occupying this mansion. Why should this be any different?

Allie replied, "Everything else that we have observed has been factual and believable. There were bodies, graves, treasures, and even strange spirits, but there has never been something that we could not explain or understand. How do you think that we will be able to tell others about this time trip? No one will believe us unless we actually show it to them. If we don't show it, we will be the laughing stock of the history community, especially the professors."

After a long discussion, the two decided that they would not show anyone the time travel method that Nathan had discovered. Without telling that they'd actually been there, they would tell the details of how life existed in the 1850s. The fascinating part of this experience was that they could now tell the history and occurrences of an actual antebellum plantation. They could present the details just like they had actually been there, which they had. The details and observations that they would tell others would be so very accurate that everyone would wonder where they secured their information.

After breakfast, both of the reporters headed to their individual studies, where they secured paper and pen and began recording their own findings of their travels. Allison had pages to write about the functioning of the mansion, along with the slaves teaching her how to cook their own favorite dishes. Marley was more zoned in on writing about the physical attributes of the plantation. He was able to meet with several of the slave men and could report their feelings about their situation and how they were being treated. As Marley considered the ramifications of the entire visit, he came to the conclusion that it was best that he and Allie had returned home when they did. He did not want to enter into any conversations that were too detailed about the Greenwell's political feelings or what he had been questioning the slaves about. He had learned all that was needed, and it had been time for them to return home.

The word leaked out about the Robbins having new and interesting facts concerning the Greenwell mansion, along with information about the actual life on a Southern plantation. Marley and Allie were both invited to give lectures on several university campuses, as well as to several community service organizations. It was extremely difficult for these speakers to present their facts without disclosing that they had actually been there. They both decided upon a "what if" approach. They would start their lecture by stating, "What if you could actually visit a working plantation of the 1800s?" This way everyone could imagine that they had been present themselves.

The maintenance of Marley and Allison's secret was more than they could bear. They had to tell someone, or they would just explode. The couple had a dear friend who was the chairman of the history department at a university. He had written several books concerning the antebellum South. Besides being a close friend, he was someone that they could trust completely. An appointment was made for them to meet with him in his office.

The Robbins were both quite nervous about sharing their knowledge about their time travel, with him or with anyone. They did, however, manage to come clean with their story about visiting the old mansion. The facts were difficult for their friend, Dr. Ames, to understand. He knew these historians for many years, and they had always acted, thought, and reported in a logical, orderly manner. This was something quite different. Dr. Ames admitted that it was difficult for him to believe their outlandish story. He would, however, be happy to travel to their home and see the phenomenon for himself. This way he could either have the two committed to a nut farm or he could help them promote the evidence of their findings. Dr. Ames was an elderly professor who had been suffering for years with a bad heart. He was not about to tarnish his reputation by telling of something with which he was not personally familiar.

The Robbins decided to invite Dr. Ames to come to their home and they would show him their hard-to-believe findings. They required Dr. Ames to sign a legal statement that he would not disclose the details, nor the founders, of this discovery to anyone. He gladly signed the papers because he wanted to see this time travel device for himself.

CHAPTER 9

The day finally arrived for Dr. Ames' visit to the finely restored mansion where Marley and Allison resided. He was graciously greeted at the door and shown to the kitchen, where they all sat and had a cup of coffee.

Dr. Ames began the conversation by saying, "You two are my closest and dearest friends. I would like to share something with you that is very private for me. I have been told by my doctors that I only have a couple of months to live. My heart is rapidly giving out."

Allie gasped and said, "Tell us that isn't the truth."

Dr. Ames assured them that he was correct about his diagnosis. He said, "If your story is correct, I want to see the facts before I die. There will be plenty of historians after I am gone, but I want to see something that will really knock my socks off so I can die without my boots on."

Marley explained the details about the time warp, even the facts that led up to their discovery. He told Dr. Ames about the metal sphere that had to be oriented toward the north for the entrance to the time warp to open.

Dr. Ames had one large request to make before they showed him the hidden closet and the stairway leading into the past. He wanted to descend the stairway by himself, unaccompanied by anyone. If he were to be allowed to view this astonishing phenomenon, he chose to do it by himself. Additionally, Dr. Ames wanted to be in possession of the metal sphere at all times.

Since there were no objections to his requests, Dr. Ames was led into the bedroom which was once occupied by Nathan Greenwell. The three secured the metal sphere and handed it to Dr. Ames. He had been instructed about turning the N on the sphere to face north.

When the doctor entered the small closet, he carefully oriented the N to face to the north. The floor began to rumble and an opening appeared, through which he could pass. Below the opening was a stairway that led to the lower room of the old Greenwell mansion. Dr. Ames could easily view servants and family members milling around in the adjacent rooms. The Robbins' story was true. It was just like they had reported.

Dr. Ames grasped the metal sphere securely, which appeared to be the object that activated the time warp. He headed, alone, down the stairway. Halfway down he looked back and called to Marley and Allison, "I now realize that all that you have told me is true. I have a very short time to live and since I have no family, I choose to live out my final days with those of whom I have studied and written."

As he reached the bottom step of the descent, he took the metal sphere and reoriented the N so that it would not point north. A rumbling again occurred, and the stairway disappeared. The access in the floor of the closet then became completely sealed up. There was no way that their friend could be rescued from the past. It was his desire. What better way to spend your final days then where and how you chose?

Marley called the local police and reported all of the details about his friend's disappearance. When the authorities arrived, they could find no evidence of any time travel device, nor could they find evidence that Dr. Ames had ever been there. They certainly did not believe the fantastic story that Marley and Allie told them. The entire case was swept under the rug and listed as a fanciful tale that had been told by two dreamer historians.

Back at the university, Dr. Ames had left a note on his desk. It read, "I have lived my life in search of history. Now that I have found it, I plan to spend my final days in its enjoyment."